Danny Is Afraid Of The Dark

NIGEL SNELL

Hamish Hamilton · London

The sun was going down.
It would soon be dark.

Danny didn't like the night.
He was afraid of the dark.

Mummy called Danny and gave him
his cup of hot milk.
Then she told him to go upstairs
and get ready for bed.

Danny was scared.

Danny turned on the bathroom light, washed his hands and face and cleaned his teeth . . .

... Then he ran into his bedroom and jumped right across the room onto his bed. Just in case there was something underneath!

Soon Mummy came in and turned off the light.
But a narrow strip of light still came through the curtain.

Suddenly Danny saw a huge bat, with
terrible teeth, hanging on the back
of the door.

Then he saw a horrible goblin
sitting on his chair.

Help! Help! Help! Help! Help! Help!

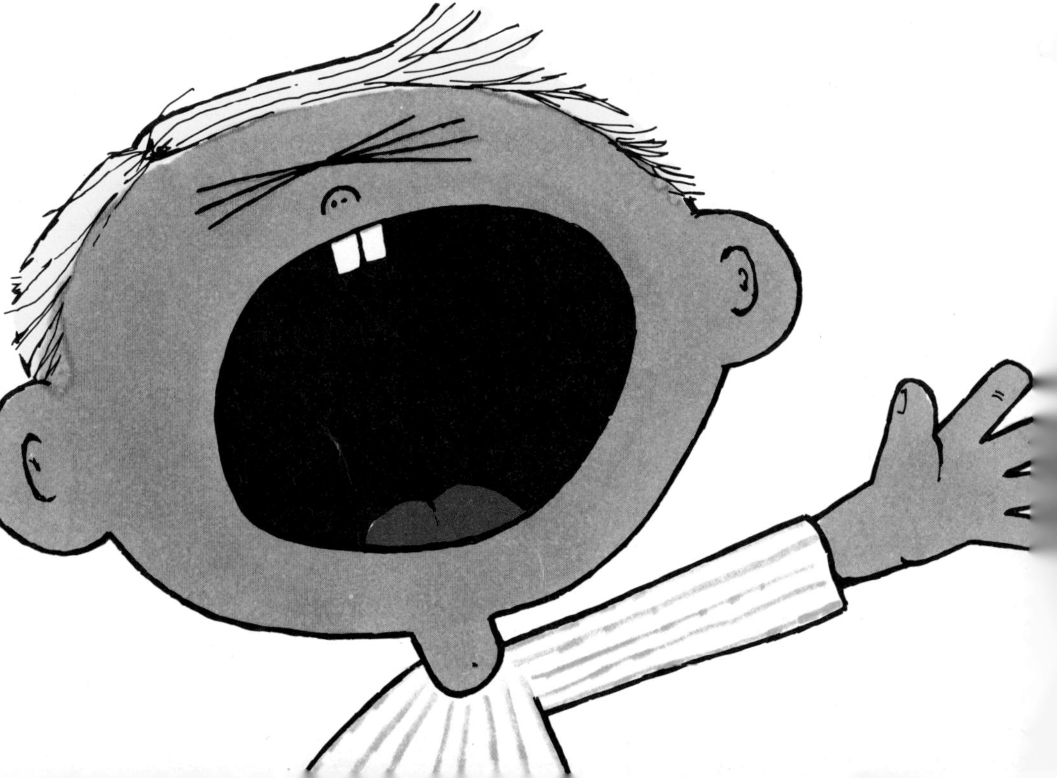

Help!

Help!

Help!

Help!

Help!

he screamed.

Mummy came running in and turned
on the light.
'What on earth is the matter?' she said.

Danny pointed to the bat and the goblin.
But when he looked again, the bat had
turned into his dressing-gown and
the goblin was just a pile of clothes.

'You are a silly billy', said Mummy. 'Fancy being frightened of your own clothes. You just imagined the bat and goblin.'
Danny smiled and felt better.

And the bat and goblin went sadly away because they knew Danny didn't believe in them any more.

Hardback edition first published in Great Britain 1982 by
Hamish Hamilton Children's Books
Garden House, 57–59 Long Acre, London WC2E 9JZ
Copyright © 1982 by Nigel Snell
All Rights Reserved

Reprinted 1983

Paperback edition first published 1985

British Library Cataloguing in Publication Data
Snell, Nigel
Danny is afraid of the dark
I. Title
823'.914[J]   PZ7
ISBN 0-241-10792-X (hardback)
ISBN 0-241-11459-4 (paperback)

Printed in Great Britain by
Cambus Litho, East Kilbride